Rebecca Rolland

PRESSURE

An Activ8r Adventure

Rebecca Rolland holds an MFA in creative writing and has published fiction including *Velocity*. She is a Harvard lecturer, speech pathologist, and author of *The Art of Talking with Children*, which has been translated into 11 languages. Her work explores how technology changes our world. Rebecca lives in Boston with her family.

First published by Gemma in 2026.

www.gemmamedia.org

Printed in the United States of America

978-1-956476-57-6

Library of Congress Cataloging-in-Publication Data

Names: Rolland, Rebecca author
Title: Pressure / Rebecca Rolland.
Description: Boston : Gemma, 2026. | Summary: Robotics student Lucy Brick must unite her friends to save her city from a killer storm caused by technology that manipulates the weather. Provided by publisher.
Identifiers: LCCN 2026008002 (print) | LCCN 2026008003 (ebook) | ISBN 9781956476576 paperback | ISBN 9781956476583 epub
Subjects: CYAC: Robotics | Artificial intelligence | Science projects | Weather | Friendship | LCGFT: Novels
Classification: LCC PZ7.1.R6648 Pr 2026 (print) | LCC PZ7.1.R6648 (ebook)
LC record available at https://lccn.loc.gov/2026008002
LC ebook record available at https://lccn.loc.gov/2026008003

Cover by Laura Shaw Design
Illustrations by Sophie Rolland

Named after the brightest star in the Northern Crown, Gemma is a nonprofit organization that helps new readers acquire English language literacy skills with relevant, engaging books, eBooks, and audiobooks. Always original, never adapted, these stories introduce adults and young adults to the life-changing power of reading.

Open Door

To my family, for their humor, love,
and nonstop inspiration

Chapter One

Lucy James cheered. Her two robots raced around the science lab.

"Go on, Little Leaf! Go, Happy Dancer!"

Lucy was a college student studying robotics in New York City. She'd built these robots herself. She stood on a chair, her heart beating fast. Mike, her supervisor, paced in circles beside her. He was tall and wore big black glasses. He was excited, too, as he watched her robots zoom across the lab floor.

Lucy had covered the floor of the lab with sand, pebbles, and sticks. That made the race tough. Little Leaf, the taller robot, was faster and sped ahead of Happy Dancer.

Little Leaf was three feet tall and made mostly of metal. His plastic arms creaked when he walked. His expressions shifted from happy to sad. Happy Dancer was shorter with a round body. He spun in fast circles. His metal wheels clicked as he moved. Lucy bounced with energy as she used the remote control to guide them. Happy Dancer was catching up. He sped up, blinking his robotic eyes.

The robots raced on the last lap, neck and neck. Neither robot had crashed yet. But Lucy was still nervous. This race in the lab was a big piece of her final project, but there was more to do. She had to show Mike they worked both indoors and outside. Outside would be harder. The real world had tons of complicated obstacles. To make a robot function, you needed to help it "see" busy streets, tree stumps, and sewer grates. It had to expect the unexpected. You needed to let it learn from its environment. She had to succeed if she wanted to graduate. And she had to graduate to become a real scientist.

"Come on, you two," Lucy called as Little Leaf pulled ahead. "Keep it up!"

When the robots finally stopped, Lucy turned to Mike. "They did great, didn't they?"

Mike smiled and nodded. He touched Little Leaf's plastic arm and patted Happy Dancer on the head. "They sure did."

Lucy grinned. "Does that mean we can test them outside now?"

With a tired look, Mike ran a hand through his blond hair. Mike was a top engineer who helped students on the side. He specialized in neural networks, or making "brains" for robots. Ideally, robots would learn and make decisions on their own. "You've done an amazing job. Still, I'm not sure they're ready for the real world."

Lucy frowned. "I think they are. Let me show you." She pulled out her notes and showed Mike the many tests the robots had passed. They could climb, jump, and roll over obstacles. They had made impressive progress. The algorithms she had programmed were working well.

"They've passed every test perfectly," she said.

Mike smiled. "OK, you win. You can try them outside."

"Are you sure?"

"Let's see how they do," Mike said. "But be careful. You know they can't get dirty or wet. That could ruin them."

"I'll be careful, I promise."

Lucy was very happy for the rest of the day. She had been working with Little Leaf and Happy Dancer for months. It was part of her degree in cognitive computing, a field of science that tried to give robots the power to think like humans. Now she would finally be able to test her robots in the real world. It was a great moment for her.

At the same time, Lucy was worried. A small voice inside told her she needed to be careful. She knew things could go badly wrong with robots. She loved science—it was her life— but she knew it wasn't always good. Or safe.

A few months before, she and her friend Julia had learned about the Activ8rs, a global organization that did dangerous experiments using science and robotics. She had stopped their evil plan to turn delivery drivers into part-robots by implanting computer chips in their brains.

But Lucy knew the Activ8rs were still out there in the world. She and her friends had promised to find their victims and help them.

What were the Activ8rs up to now? she wondered. Where were they making trouble? It could be anywhere, in any country, even in the city where she lived.

The idea made her shiver. She tried to focus on her own project and stay calm.

Chapter Two

At five o'clock, Lucy took Little Leaf outside. It was rush hour in Manhattan. The heavy rain made it tough to walk. Cars honked noisily. Bikes swerved across Fifth Avenue. In the distance, a siren squalled.

Lucy had planned to let Little Leaf explore, but the rain made that impossible. She couldn't risk ruining him. Seeing a vacant bench on the sidewalk, she sat down. She placed Little Leaf beside her. Little Leaf had arms that looked like leaves and enormous eyes. Usually, he had a cheerful smile, but now his eyes crossed. Maybe he missed Happy Dancer.

"Come on, Little Leaf." Lucy took out a special plastic cover and draped it over him. "We'll wait till it's dry. Afterward, we'll test you on the street."

After ten minutes, the rain finally stopped. Lucy set Little Leaf down. Crowds crammed the streets. A food truck selling tacos parked at the corner. Soon, a line snaked down the block. Kids on electric scooters zoomed past. A dog on a leash barked and ran toward them. Little Leaf sped up, his motor whirring as he scooted ahead.

A woman with a stroller bumped into Little Leaf's wheel. Lucy scooped him up, cradling him. His wheels purred. His programming drove him forward, not his feelings. Still, she imagined he *could* have feelings, inside his circuits.

"Let's find a quieter place," she said, "and try again."

Lucy tested three different streets. Each time, she ran into new problems. Motorbikes sped down the sidewalks. People with briefcases rushed by, banging into her. Little Leaf scooted forward, backed up, and spun. Probably his sensors were overloaded. He couldn't process so much new data.

"This isn't working." Lucy wiped her eyes. "We need a new plan."

Chapter Three

Over the next days, Lucy searched for the perfect spot in New York City for Little Leaf and Happy Dancer. She brought them to Central Park, a place she loved. The park felt peaceful after the bustle of city streets. The air smelled of oak trees and blossoms. Still, every time she went out, kids on scooters kept colliding with her robots. The robots had a hard time rolling. She had built them to work on smooth city streets, not in grassy parks.

Lucy returned to Mike's office. A heavy weight filled her chest. "I only have a month left before the deadline," she said. "Right now, it feels like everything is falling apart."

Mike scratched his chin. "You could keep looking around New York," he said. "Or you could test out a new place. There's a big world out there, with many different challenges. In the end, your robots will need to adapt."

Lucy furrowed her brow. Mike was right, but she didn't like to admit it. Robots usually did well with basic problems. But when the problems were unexpected, they had a hard time.

Say your robot dog needs to get your slippers. Its wheels are stuck. That's easy enough to fix. You need to get its wheels unstuck.

But what if the robot gets confused? Maybe it picks up a shoebox instead of your slippers. That's a harder problem to fix.

"So, what do you think I should do?" Lucy asked.

Mike shrugged. "Don't ask me. You're the creative one."

That night, Lucy called her friend Mandy. Lucy hadn't seen her in months. Mandy was a *dliv*, a delivery driver who had been partly turned into a robot. They had gone on a great adventure together. Lucy had helped Mandy and other dlivs reclaim their freedom and become fully human. Now, she needed Mandy's help.

"What do you think Mike meant?" Lucy asked. "Where else could I try?"

"Wait a second." Mandy's face lit up. "My dad lives in Cooperstown, in the countryside of New York. It's super chill. You could come stay with me and test Little Leaf there."

Lucy's heart pounded. "I don't have much money, and I need to finish my work."

"My dad's a scientist. He could give you great advice."

What if Lucy needed her tools or equipment? She called Mike to get his take.

"Try it," Mike said, "but be careful. If the robots break, you're back to square one."

Lucy couldn't afford to start again. Her scholarship was running out.

That afternoon, Lucy packed up Little Leaf and Happy Dancer. She buckled them into her car like little kids, double-checking that they were secure. Traffic packed the roads to

Cooperstown. As she got closer, beautiful oaks and aspens lined the road.

When she finally arrived, Mandy was waiting outside.

"I'm so glad you're here," Mandy said. Mandy had straight brown hair in a ponytail and brown eyes. She looked nothing like Lucy. Still, Lucy often imagined they were sisters. As they unloaded the robots, Lucy felt warmth spread in her chest. Inside, Mandy's dad, Billy, greeted them. Dressed in a black leather jacket and worn jeans, he had a grizzled look, but his smile was warm.

"So, who are these little fellas?" Billy eyed the robots with interest.

Lucy grinned. "I hope they can help blind people one day."

Billy nodded. "That's a great goal. But remember, the outdoors is full of surprises."

"I know." Lucy's stomach knotted. "Rain and wet ground are my biggest worries. But I have to try."

Billy frowned. "Usually, I'd be optimistic, but with the recent weather patterns...."

"What do you mean?" Lucy asked.

"The weather here has been weird," Mandy said.

"Weird? Like how?" Lucy probed.

Mandy shrugged. "It's been… unpredictable. Maybe it's nothing."

Chapter Four

The next morning, Lucy decided to take a walk in Cooperstown. It was much quieter than New York City. The streets were tranquil and almost deserted. The air felt cool and crisp. She couldn't imagine a better place to test her robots. She'd start with Little Leaf.

"Let's go, Little Leaf," she said. She took the small robot and stepped into the open.

Overhead, the sun blazed. Dark clouds rolled in. Rain poured from the sky. Startled, Lucy pulled up her hood. Soon, it was hailing. Ice pellets bounced on the ground. Lucy gasped. She'd never seen such a sudden ice storm. She stuck Little Leaf in his container.

She hurried back to Mandy's house. By the time she arrived, the sun shone bright, like nothing had happened. Lucy waited, then tried walking to a nearby street. In the span of fifteen minutes, it turned cloudy, sunny, raining, and snowy. The snow froze her face. Her feet sloshed in her shoes. Her fingertips felt like icicles.

"This is bizarre," Lucy grumbled, clutching Little Leaf. Her heart pounded hard. She couldn't get her robot wet. Her project could be ruined. She'd never graduate in time. She'd disappoint her family and herself.

Back at Mandy's house, she set Little Leaf next to Happy Dancer. Taking an umbrella, she asked Mandy to go for a walk with her. Mandy agreed.

As they walked, Mandy talked non-stop. "I've had a hard time making my deliveries. I can't decide whether to wear rain boots or sneakers. I keep getting soaked. I have to change clothes three times a day. My bike is rusted. If this keeps up, I might have to stop working."

"What's happening?" Lucy asked.

"I'm not sure." Mandy frowned. "I ignored it, but it's only getting worse."

When they returned, Lucy turned on the TV. On the screen, a woman was reporting from a football game. The sky filled with clouds. Rain drummed, and the wind started howling. The reporter yanked out an umbrella.

"The game has to stop," the reporter said, as her umbrella strained against the wind. "This weather is out of control!"

Lucy shut the TV off. Normally, she adored science. It let her ask questions and understand how the world worked. She especially loved questions about machine perception. How can computers and robots best interpret data from the outside world? How could we help them "hear" and "smell" and "see?" But how could she finish her project with the weather so strange? Maybe she should go back to New York City. But that would mean leaving Mandy. She checked the weather on her phone.

An alert popped up: "Warning: New York City has been experiencing rapid weather shifts. Each neighborhood may have different weather. Exercise caution."

Lucy showed the alert to Mandy.

"That's even weirder," Mandy said. "It's happening in New York City, too?"

Lucy nodded. "I need to test the robots outdoors, but it's way too risky. Hey, I have an idea. What if we could *fix* the weather problem?"

Mandy's eyes widened. "You think we can fix the weather?"

"We have to try at least, don't we?"

"But how?" Mandy asked.

"We need to identify the trigger. Then, we can see what created this problem."

Mandy agreed. "But what could the trigger be?"

Chapter Five

The next day, Lucy and Mandy went outside, determined to figure out why the weather was shifting so fast. It was a glorious sunny morning, but they left the robots behind. They packed snacks and weather gear. Lucy carried her favorite green notebook. She used it to record her questions and ideas.

As they walked, Lucy remembered what Mike always said: "If you don't have good questions, how can you get good answers?" Creating the right questions would be key. This was definitely an adaptive challenge, not a technical one.

"Why has the weather gone haywire?" Lucy asked Mandy as they walked.

Mandy sighed. "I don't have the faintest idea."

"We'll crack this case. Trust me," Lucy said. Opening her notebook, she scribbled, "Why has the weather become unstable?" and "How can we stabilize it?"

Mandy peered over her shoulder. "How about adding a third question?" Using Lucy's pen, she wrote, "How to stabilize the weather—fast?"

Lucy laughed. "That's a simple way of putting it."

A woman on rollerblades whizzed past. She wore big headphones and had a golden retriever on a leash, running behind her. The woman crashed into the bench where Lucy and Mandy sat. Her keys and phone spilled out of her bag. Her dog skidded to a halt beside her.

"Oh, sorry," the woman exclaimed.

"It's OK." Lucy grabbed the woman's phone and keys. "Here you go."

The woman thanked Lucy and pocketed her keys. She clicked a button on her phone. Her wristwatch chimed. In an instant, thunder boomed, lightning split the sky, and a downpour started. The woman skated away. Drenched, Lucy gasped, and Mandy clutched her arm.

"We should have brought umbrellas!" Lucy exclaimed.

"How were we supposed to know?" Mandy asked.

They dashed across the street to the closest café. They settled into a booth, trying to dry off. Gazing out the window, Lucy noticed joggers and bikers sporting similar watches. They kept pressing buttons. Some spoke into their devices. Lucy checked her phone again.

A new alert popped up: "Warning! Severe weather imminent."

"More severe weather?" Lucy groaned.

A clap of thunder shook the café. Mandy's phone rang.

Frowning, Mandy handed Lucy the phone.

"My dad wants to talk to you," Mandy said.

"You need to come back soon." Billy's voice boomed over the phone. "Your robots are beeping nonstop. I can't get them to calm down."

Chapter Six

"What's wrong with your robots?" Mandy asked.

"I'm not sure," Lucy said. "They usually beep when their power reserves are low. Also, I programmed them to beep to signal danger or any major shifts in air pressure."

"Like what kind of danger?" Mandy asked.

"If there's a sudden threat or a major shift in the air."

"I hope there's no big danger."

"I'm sure there's not." Lucy started to regret her decision to come to Cooperstown.

"I need to get a move on with my deliveries," Mandy said. "I'm behind schedule."

Lucy and Mandy headed back. Every five minutes, the conditions shifted. A storm appeared. The sky blazed with lightning. Soon, the storm cleared, and the sky grew overcast. Hail fell, pelting their faces and arms.

"What in the world is happening?" Lucy winced. Her head was throbbing, and she shielded her notebook with her bag. Ahead of them, a jogger came to a quick stop. He fiddled with his wristwatch. The hail stopped, and the sun shone bright once more.

"That's so bizarre," Lucy said.

"What?" Mandy asked.

"That guy just pressed a button, and the weather transformed."

As they rounded the corner onto Mandy's street, a runner sprinted past. He tapped a button on his smartwatch, and a downpour began. Lucy gasped. The rain had a strangely acidic taste, and she recoiled.

"We need to get out of here!" Lucy yelled.

Back at Mandy's house, they both took towels and dried off. Lucy needed to finish her project, but how could she, with this chaos swirling around her?

Inside, Little Leaf and Happy Dancer whirled in a frenzied dance. Their nonstop clicking and chirping sounds filled the air. Overhead, lights flickered. The room plunged into darkness. Billy, Mandy's dad, hovered over the robots.

"I'm baffled," Billy said. "They won't quiet down."

"And what's happening with the power surges?" Mandy asked.

Billy shrugged. "Maybe they're related to the storms."

Lucy leaned over her robots. They were making a strange pattern of clicks. Three fast ones. A pause. Two slow ones. How strange. She hadn't programmed them to do that. Happy Dancer's screen stayed blank. Little Leaf's screen glowed a bright eerie green. His screen displayed a message: "Return to boss. Now."

"What's that?" Mandy asked, peeking over Lucy's shoulder.

"It's nothing." Lucy flushed. She had constructed these robots and programmed them. They weren't conscious, the way people were. Little Leaf's screen showed a map. The map flashed with arrows directing them down Cooperstown streets.

"It's probably a minor glitch," Billy said as the lights flickered faster. "Did you build these robots totally from scratch?"

Lucy gulped. "Almost. I took one shortcut."

"What sort of shortcut?" Billy asked.

"I borrowed a computer chip from an old friend." Robby wasn't exactly a friend. He was the scientist behind the Activ8rs. He was brilliant and had wild ideas. "He assured me it would work without fail. I built the robots using that as a base."

"You better ask Robby then," Billy said.

"Maybe." Lucy nestled the robots. The last time she'd talked to Robby, he'd yelled. People were making robots without his approval, he said. "But first, let's follow the map."

"Sorry, I can't join you." Mandy pointed to the window. The sun looked like a fireball, high in the sky. "With the weather this calm, I can ride my bike. It's time to make up for my missed deliveries. I have to go."

"I'll go alone then," Lucy said. "At least the weather seems more stable."

"Maybe not for long," Billy warned, handing her a huge golf umbrella.

"Thanks." Lucy smiled. She covered the robots with plastic, took the umbrella, and ventured out. The robots' map guided her through the streets. Who was this "boss?" Where were they headed? She strode faster. On the first street, she saw a young woman walking a leashed Dalmatian. The woman clicked a button on her watch. The sky transformed, awash in clouds.

"Hey," Lucy called out. "What's that watch?"

"Haven't you heard of the Personal Weather Changer?" the woman asked. She introduced herself as Susan Bartlett.

Lucy shook her head.

"It's the latest craze," Susan said. "But it's super expensive, and it guzzles power. The battery drains way too fast. What a shame."

"What does it do?"

"What doesn't it do?" Susan retorted. Shrugging, she clicked the button again. A purple haze enveloped the sky. "It's been malfunctioning lately, though. I've been trying to keep the weather sunny, but the watch keeps losing power. I need to speak with the boss about it."

"Wait, what? That watch changes the weather?"

"It's supposed to." Susan sighed. "It should be a simple algorithm. But it's filled with glitches. There must be a programming error. Everyone's weather is clashing. That's causing storms. Do you think you could get some coders on it?"

"I'm not a computer scientist," Lucy said.

"Oh, I'm sorry." Susan smiled. "You looked like one."

Susan hurried off, tugging her dog behind her. Lucy stood still. Her robots chirped. Both screens blared the urgent message: "See the boss."

"Where is this boss?" Lucy asked, but Susan had already left.

Happy Dancer's screen glowed green. An arrow pointed left, down a dark alley.

"OK, robots." Lucy gritted her teeth. "Let's move."

Chapter Eight

Striding forward, Lucy followed the robots down the alley. Happy Dancer's screen showed an arrow pointing down. Where was "down" exactly?

"Let's see," she muttered, as she tested wide streets, then narrower ones. The arrow stayed on *down,* no matter how she turned.

At the end of the alley lay a sewer grate. Shivering, Lucy drew closer.

"I hope you don't mean we should go in *there,*" Lucy said. Happy Dancer beeped louder. Little Leaf twirled in circles like an excited kid. Did those robots want to go underground? Lucy paused. She *really* disliked dark, creepy spaces. But she had to follow their instructions. That was the only way to find the boss. Shaking, she pried the grate open. In each arm, she took one robot. She climbed down a long ladder and landed with a thud.

The robots clicked their wheels.

Underground, she found a somber street. A few bare lights flickered. The place reeked of rats and dirty socks. Lucy squinched her nose. At the hallway's end, in the shadows, something—or someone—was making a scrabbling noise.

"We need a solution," a man was saying. "This is out of control."

Lucy tiptoed down the hallway. Her phone was out of service. How could she contact Mandy? Her left foot cramped, and she shook it out. She had to figure out what the robots needed. Even if it was dangerous, she had to follow them.

At the end of the hallway stood a huge white door. Lucy knocked.

"Who are you?" a young man asked, creaking the door open. Behind him, Lucy saw a group of people about her age, typing on laptops. The room glowed with the light of so many screens. Maps on the laptops showed shifting weather patterns. One screen had a swirl of green, and another one showed a dark purple haze.

"Who are *you?*" Lucy asked.

"This space is private," the man snapped. He was tall and lanky, dressed in a flashy business suit. He introduced himself as Tom Templeman. "You're not allowed here."

As her robots chirped louder, Lucy pressed past him. Loud shouts rose from the room as workers complained.

"Where is your supervisor?" Lucy called out.

"What supervisor?" a young woman asked. Behind her, Lucy noticed a metal structure resembling a telephone booth.

"My robots insist on seeing the boss," Lucy said. "So where is he?"

No one answered. Lucy heard the sound of hurried footsteps. She turned. It was Susan, racing down the hall.

"I need to charge my WeatherPal," Susan called. "It's an emergency! My phone charger at home is too weak."

"Now, Susan," the woman in front of Lucy said. "This isn't the right time.

The power grid is already disrupted. Too many people are charging their watches. They are creating a surge."

"I need to charge it." Susan said. "Or it will lose its connection and stop working."

Before Lucy could ask anything else, Susan rushed to the booth.

"Hold on," Lucy exclaimed, her mind reeling. The robots' noises escalated. Happy Dancer spun out of her grasp. "What is this booth you're talking about?"

"It's like a power station," Susan called back. "It's a super powerful hub."

"OK. So how does it operate?" Lucy asked.

Susan didn't answer. Lucy shut her eyes. She remembered the booth the dlivs had used. They'd shrunk their ear canals. That's what made the charging chopsticks fit. But that booth didn't resemble this one. And she didn't see anyone here with small ear canals.

"It will be quick," Susan reassured her. "You can have your turn next."

"We'll call security," Tom said. "No outsiders allowed."

"But I need answers," Lucy insisted, her voice rising. Banging and crashing rose from inside the booth. Susan called out, "I'm so cold!"

Lucy stepped closer to the booth. The closer she drew, the louder her robots droned.

"Find the boss NOW," Happy Dancer's screen blared. "Emergency."

A model number was stamped on the booth: Booth 112A. That was odd. Could this be the type of booth Robby had used? And why the number 112A? Could there be over a hundred booths like this? Lucy leaned in closer.

"I'm getting overheated!" Susan called. "And drenched!"

Lucy pounded on the booth's door. Could the boss be with Susan? What if he was forcing her to talk? She felt a tap from behind. It was Tom, his brow furrowed.

"There's a hurricane on its way," he said. "No outsiders allowed."

"Just give me a minute, OK?" Lucy begged.

She yanked open the booth door. Susan was seated inside, plugging her

WeatherPal into the wall. An overhead light blazed. A sign flashed "Weather Cycle Finished."

"Well, that's a relief." Susan stood. She wore a plastic poncho, and her hair was dripping wet. "I thought it would never end."

"What would never end?" Lucy turned to see Happy Dancer and Little Leaf rolling toward Susan's chair. "Charging started," a sign on the booth proclaimed. "Wait for full cycle."

"Hold on, robots." Her heart pounded. She couldn't let her robots charge here. What if the network stole their data? It wouldn't be her own anymore. Her whole project could be compromised. She could even fail out of school.

"I don't think this system is safe," she told Susan. "We've got to be careful."

"Sorry, I've got to go." Susan handed Lucy her poncho. "Take this." She scribbled on a piece of paper. "Here's my number if you want to call."

Chapter Nine

Taking the poncho, Lucy covered the two robots. Their batteries had almost drained. She plugged them both in. They beeped and swerved as they charged.

After twenty minutes, the weather calmed down. The lights flickered back on. Both robots whizzed around. Their batteries had filled. Lucy craned open the Booth door.

Four workers stood outside, hands on their hips. Tom, their leader, stood at the front.

"This is a private office," Tom said. "Who told you about us?"

"The robots," Lucy said.

"The robots?" Tom's eyebrows shot up.

"Never mind." Lucy straightened her shoulders. "What is this booth? And what's this charging method? It's so fast."

"A full charge requires a complete weather cycle," Tom explained. "Sunshine, rain, storms, and clouds. That's how the watches gain power."

"The Booth is like a super-charger," another worker added. "It's way more powerful than home chargers. That's why people flock here."

"OK," Lucy managed. "And who's the boss?"

"I should be asking you that." Tom gave a sly smile. "You know Robby, don't you?"

Lucy gasped. "Is Robby behind this?"

"The WeatherPal was his idea," Tom admitted. "Way back. But he didn't think it through. Now, he's scrambling to fix the power grid."

"Too many people charge devices at the same time," a worker said. "It's straining the city's power supply. Soon, we won't have power for our homes or schools."

"That's awful," Lucy exclaimed. "Can't you force them to stop?"

Tom shrugged. "It's beyond our control. Everybody wants custom weather. Their changes take lots of energy. No one is making rules. It's a free-for-all."

Lucy frowned. The erratic weather patterns. Susan charging her device.

The power surges. She turned to Happy Dancer and Little Leaf. They never spun around so fast. "What's also strange is these robots," she said.

"What about them?" Tom asked.

"I don't know how they knew to come here." She picked them up. "And why they even needed a charge. Normally, my charging routine is enough." She paused, waiting for Tom. He didn't speak. "There's only one thing to do. I'll call Robby."

"Maybe best to wait out the hurricane first," Tom said.

Lucy shook her head. "No time for that."

She grabbed both robots. She dashed outside, fighting the rain and wind. Bikers and joggers rushed for shelter. The huge oak trees creaked and swayed. She tried calling Robby, but he didn't answer. She texted him instead.

"Out of office," his auto-reply read. "Try in an hour."

"Are you OK?" she texted Mandy. "Where are you?"

"I've had to stop my deliveries," Mandy texted back. "My bike's battery is depleted."

"So where are you?" Lucy wrote back.

"I'm home."

Lucy raced back, arms aching.

"I'm so glad you made it," Mandy said. "Are the robots OK?"

"For now," Lucy replied. "But listen, there's a more serious story."

Billy came downstairs. Lucy told them both what had happened.

"That's risky," Billy said. "You know the saying about a butterfly flapping its wings?"

"What about it?" Lucy asked.

"Even small shifts can have big effects," he explained. "Imagine a butterfly flaps its wings in one city. That might end up causing a tornado many miles away."

"Right now, I'm worried about the power grid," Lucy explained. "What if there is a power outage? If people can't cool their houses or keep food cold?" She sighed. "I'll call Robby again."

Chapter Ten

An hour later, Lucy reached Robby. "Was the WeatherPal your idea?" she asked. She was sitting in Mandy's kitchen with a plate of cookies. Her robots perched beside her.

"I didn't manufacture the Weather-Pals," Robby said. "I only came up with the idea. Someone in another company handled the production."

"But that's a terrible idea," Lucy said. "Think about the mess it's causing."

"It was an experiment." He sighed. "I never thought they'd become so popular."

"What about the power crisis?" Lucy asked.

"I'm trying my best to stop it," Robby said. "I'm working with the energy companies. I'm sorry—I didn't think things would get out of control."

Lucy told him about her trip underground. She asked about the charging booth.

"I don't know about a Booth like that," Robby said.

"It has a model number," Lucy added. "Like your Booth did."

"So?"

"Where did you get the Booth?" Lucy asked. "And what my robots' computer chips?"

The Booth, he said, came from a manufacturer called New Life. Their factory made computer chips. To know more, she'd have to contact them.

A burst of lightning lit the windows. Lucy jumped. The lights flickered.

"Sorry," she told Robby. "I think we're losing power."

"You're in Cooperstown, right?" Robby asked.

"Yes."

"Have you been following the news? There's a major storm coming. It's unlike anything the city has ever seen. And it's manmade."

"You're joking."

"Why would I joke about like that?"

"But a manmade storm could be way worse than a real one."

Robby agreed. "And I don't see how anyone can prevent it."

"I could try." Lucy clenched her fists.

"How?"

"I'll have to think."

"Good luck. If anyone can do it, you can."

That night, Lucy huddled with Mandy and Billy and discussed what to do. What if she could create personal WeatherPals? They would only change the weather above people's heads. They would be safer. The weather chaos would disappear. Plus, they'd be such cool gadgets that everyone would want one.

Maybe the WeatherPal company would come to her. "How did you build these?" they'd ask. That could be the start of a great career. She decided not to breathe a word of it to Robby. He'd try to take over, as usual.

Chapter Eleven

After making her decision, Lucy switched on the news.

"The storm is still lurking off the coast," the TV reporter said. "We have only three days before it hits the city with full force. Time is slipping away, and there's no way to stop it."

Lucy turned off the news. She had to act fast. How could she mass-produce new WeatherPals? Three days was not enough time. So what? Maybe she could change how the WeatherPals worked. She wouldn't need totally new devices. She could just tweak the settings. That could limit their powers.

"What do you think?" she asked Mandy.

"Not bad," Mandy said. "But why not push for a full ban on Weather-Pals?"

"We'd need to ask the government. That would take time. There would be lots of red tape," Lucy explained.

"True, but it would be safer."

"Right now, we need a quicker solution," Lucy said.

"OK. But still, we need a Weather-Pal to experiment on."

Lucy called Susan and asked to borrow her device. Susan didn't like the idea. What if her prized possession got damaged? Lucy made a promise. If the plan succeeded, she'd give Susan three extra devices for her friends.

"That sounds like an awesome deal." Susan agreed to help.

An hour later, Susan arrived with her WeatherPal. Lucy and Mandy transformed Billy's office into their lab space. It was full of tools and had lots of room to work. Billy offered advice. They worked non-stop into the night. It was hard, painstaking work. They had to be very careful. One wrong move could destroy the device. Finally, Lucy cracked open the WeatherPal. Inside lay a tiny computer chip. It had a name printed on the side. NewChip Corporation. That sounded familiar.

She scrolled through the photos on her phone.

"That's the same name as on the Booth!" she shouted. "Are these chips and the Booth connected?"

"Maybe," Mandy said. "But let's keep working."

"You're right."

They worked for three more hours. Finally, Lucy felt confident the device would work.

"Let's test it," she declared, flipping the switch. They hurried toward the lobby. She set the dial to Good Weather. A burst of flames shot up to the ceiling.

"Whoa!" Mandy yelled as Lucy scrambled, trying to stop the flames. "That's not good weather. What in the world is happening?"

"I have no idea," Lucy groaned. "The watch must be way more powerful than I thought."

She ran to shut the device off. The flames vanished as soon as they had appeared.

"Watch out," the device said in a robotic voice. "This device is for external use only."

"I guess it has a mind of its own," Lucy said, laughing. "Let's take this show outside."

"Are you sure it's safe?" Mandy asked.

"There's only one way to find out."

Chapter Twelve

Lucy and Mandy went outside to test the new WeatherPal. Lucy held her breath. Around them, joggers and cyclists zipped by, WeatherPals strapped to their wrists.

"Ready?" Mandy asked.

Lucy nodded, her fingers hovering over the Good Weather button. She pressed it, and sunlight blazed above their heads. Cardinals and sparrows flew past, chirping. The rest of the sky stayed shrouded in gray.

"Should we try the other settings?" Mandy asked.

"Definitely."

One by one, they cycled through the options. The Stormy Weather setting made a tiny storm cloud form overhead. The Calm Weather setting created a patch of serene blue sky. The Fall Weather setting infused the sky with a crisp chill.

"It's working," Lucy grinned. "It really is."

"This is incredible." Mandy pumped her fist. "We might actually be able to stop the storm. We can stop people from messing with the weather."

"And I can finally take my robots outside," Lucy added.

"What should we call these revamped devices?" Mandy asked. "We need a catchy name."

"How about MyWeatherPals?"

"Oh, I like that," Mandy said.

"But hold on. There's one snag."

"What's that?" Mandy asked.

"It's just us against thousands." Lucy pointed to the swarms of people with their weather-changing devices. "They're all changing the weather. We won't be able to avoid the storm."

Mandy lit up. "You're right. We can't expect strangers to give up their WeatherPals. But I know just the crew who would help."

She reminded Lucy about the Activ8rs, her fellow delivery drivers back in New York.

Robby had tried to transform them into robotic drones. He wanted to make them more efficient. But that made them less human. Loyal and fearless, they had banded together to stop him. They were great friends and would probably love to help. During their deliveries, they could show off the changed devices. They'd spread the word to their customers.

"We'll start a movement," Lucy said. "We'll make sure the news media catches wind of it. That way, everyone wishing to stop the storm can unite."

"Brilliant!" Mandy exclaimed.

Mandy made a flurry of calls. The Activ8rs had busy schedules. Still, they were deeply worried about the storm. When Mandy explained the plan, they agreed.

"Perfect," Lucy said. Her phone buzzed with a text. Mike was wondering when she'd be back at the lab. He asked if her project would be done soon. Robby had called ten times, demanding to know what she was up to.

"Don't leave me out," Robby texted. "I want in on the action."

Lucy was so close to being a real scientist. She couldn't let Robby steal her thunder.

"Who's texting?" Mandy asked.

"No one important." Lucy decided to ignore the calls.

Chapter Thirteen

Once the Activ8rs arrived, they had a party. Everyone gobbled down plates of smoked salmon and cream cheese, their favorites.

"This is awesome," said an Activ8r named Jim. "Tell us, how can we help?"

Lucy explained their mission. The Activ8rs would change their Weather-Pals into MyWeatherPals. Lucy would guide them. Afterward, they'd teach customers to tweak their watches. Their WeatherPals could become MyWeath-erPals, too. They would only change the weather above their own heads. People would use less power and create fewer storms.

"It won't be easy," Lucy said, "but I think it's the only solution."

"And it means we could get back to our deliveries," Mandy said.

"Will it be complicated?" Jim asked. "Will we need special tools?"

"Screwdrivers would be ideal," Lucy said. "But I doubt you have any."

"I have chopsticks." Jim smiled. "We used them for charging ourselves, remember?"

"I remember." Lucy laughed. "Those might be just what we need."

Lucy borrowed Jim's watch and the chopsticks. She was in luck. The chopsticks fit into the watch's hole perfectly. Lucy gathered the Activ8rs and showed them how to modify their devices.

Everyone had chopsticks, so they were done in no time.

Lucy switched on her two robots. They swerved around, beeping. Her phone rang with calls from Robby. She ignored them. After stopping the storm, she'd reveal everything.

"Let's go outside," she called to the Activ8rs. Their devices were now MyWeatherPals. "We'll put them to the test. We'll teach everyone we meet how help us."

Mandy asked, "What if no one wants to follow our advice?"

"All we can do is ask," Lucy said.

The Activ8rs hopped on their motorbikes and headed out into the gloomy day. Lucy shivered, breathing in the wintry chill.

"Let's get started," Jim said. He gathered the other Activ8rs. "One, two, three, go!"

In an instant, the Activ8rs powered up their modified watches.

Chapter Fourteen

Boom! A loud noise rose from the devices. *Bang!*

The Activ8rs shook. Lucy and Mandy cried out.

"What's going on?" Lucy asked. The robots whirled in circles. A message appeared on their screens: "Return to the Booth."

Lucy bent down to inspect them.

"Look at this." Jim showed his wrist to Lucy. "It keeps saying, 'Problem detected. Return to the Booth.'" His face flushed. "Our watches are destroyed! We won't be able to complete deliveries. We'll be fired from our jobs."

"And it's all your fault," another Activ8r said to Lucy, his fists clenched.

Lucy examined the MyWeatherPals. The Activ8rs were right. The devices weren't working. Now her project had failed, and her friends felt betrayed.

"Should we go back to the Booth?" Lucy whispered.

"Maybe," Mandy said. "But look."

The signal was coming from underground. Overhead, the sky was growing dark. The robots clicked and hiccupped. Happy Dancer zigzagged. Little Leaf jolted forward. Lucy and her friends sprinted to catch up.

"The Booth's signals are too strong," Lucy said. "They are stopping our devices. We need to go underground and stop them."

"But who's underground?" Mandy asked, trembling. "Do you mean Tom?"

"We're nowhere near Tom's hideout," Lucy said.

Lucy and the others followed the robots. They headed to a sewer at the end of the street. The robots circled. Their beeping rose to a fever pitch.

"We need to access the sewer," Lucy said. "We're going down."

"Are you sure?" Mandy asked, her brow furrowed.

"What if they discover the MyWeatherPals?" Jim asked. "They'll be furious."

Lucy said, "The signal is our only lead. Let's go."

They climbed down into the sewer. Around them, everything was dark. The air was thick with the smell of decay. Lucy's palms were sweaty. She clutched her robots to her chest.

"What's that?" Jim said as they reached the bottom.

"Where?" Lucy asked. At the hallway's end stood a bright door. Lucy could hear laughter and voices. She tiptoed down the hall and knocked. A young man opened and greeted them with a surprised look. His badge read "Nick, New Life Team."

"Can I help you?" Nick asked. "We weren't expecting visitors."

"We need to know the Booth signal," Lucy said. Behind Nick, rows of machines hummed. Workers gathered around monitors showing an oncoming storm. Dark clouds swirled. But the workers were clapping.

"Who are those people?" Lucy asked. "And why are they clapping?"

Nick said, "They're just excited about the coming storm."

Chapter Fifteen

Excited about the storm? Lucy gulped. "Who is New Life? Why is everyone so excited?"

Nick raised one hand. "It's complicated."

"Tell us." Her robots buzzed. She remembered the Booth had the New Life label. So did the computer chips.

Nick confessed, "We engineered the WeatherPals. We wanted to let people control the weather. It would be fun, we thought."

"You created the WeatherPals?" Lucy asked. "From scratch?"

"Not exactly," Nick hedged.

"Do you know Robby?" Lucy asked.

"We've been in contact."

Lucy faced him. "Tell me all you know."

"He also used our New Life computer chips. But Robby's WeatherPals are different. Ours use AI. We teach machines to uncover what people want. It's like they're kids in school."

"Machines decide on the weather?" Lucy asked. "Even against people's wishes?"

"Not exactly. They only predict what people want. Then they award points for picking weather patterns. That's how the effects get bigger."

"So that's how the storm happened," Lucy said.

"And how it destroyed our watches." Mandy showed her broken device to Nick.

"I see." Nick led them to the computer screens. The workers cheered, but he told them to stay quiet. "Our experiment is working. The AI systems are taking over. The problem is, its goals are different from ours. We're not in sync."

"The system wants the storm?" Lucy asked.

"No. But it likes when people have strong feelings. It notices when their hearts beat faster. And it tries to make them beat faster still."

"But now the whole city is on alert. The storm might flood Cooperstown. What if worse storms follow? We need to act fast."

"But people won't want to weaken their devices." Nick frowned. "Even if you convince a few people, it won't be enough."

Lucy's robots twirled. The workers cooed at them.

"I know," Lucy agreed. "The robots are cute. What if we tell people we need to help these robots? Stopping the storm would let them get outside. We could call it 'Set the Robots Free.'"

"Or 'Help Little Leaf and Happy Dancer,'" Mandy suggested, her eyes gleaming.

"Why not both?" Jim asked with a smile.

Nick lit up. "I can send a message to the users. But the decision still lies with them. They will have to modify their devices themselves."

"Can you tell them to meet us at the park?" Lucy asked.

Nick agreed. "I can't promise it will work. But it's worth a try."

Chapter Sixteen

Outside, rain poured. Cars swerved over flooded streets. Newscasters in ponchos waved their hands, shouting, "Imminent storm! Everyone, seek shelter!"

Lucy turned to Little Leaf and Happy Dancer. "It's not safe for you."

She stuck those robots in their containers. Then she dashed to the closest newscaster.

"Please tell everyone it's urgent." Lucy held her robots up. "We need to stop this storm. The AI system must be contained. Keep Little Leaf and Happy Dancer safe!"

"Who are these charming robots?" the newscaster asked.

Lucy outlined her plan. By converting their devices, people could stop the coming storm. All they needed were screwdrivers or chopsticks. They should come to the park to get help.

"We'll spread out across the city," Jim and the other Activ8rs said. "That way, people won't have to travel in the storm."

"That's a great idea," Lucy said.

"I'll broadcast the message," the newscaster assured them.

Lucy and the Activ8rs picked ten locations across the city. Lucy asked the newscaster to update viewers. Soon the wind picked up, howling harder.

"Cycling will be risky," Jim muttered.

"Let's risk it," Mandy said, her gaze fixed on the thunderclouds. The newscaster was already packing up.

Shivering, Lucy agreed. Her robot's beeping matched her own racing pulse.

"Failure isn't an option," she said. "If we fail, the city could flood."

Lucy and Mandy hurried toward the park entrance. They took shelter in the Visitor Center. Together, they crafted a sign that said, "Safeguard the city. Modify your WeatherPals here."

Flinging open the Visitor Center door, Lucy called, "Help save the city. Control the weather just above your head!"

A jogger slowed down. "What's this about?"

Lucy explained, waving him inside.

"It sounds complicated. I like my WeatherPal the way it is."

"Don't you want to help the city and the robots?" Lucy asked.

"I can help the city in other ways." With shrug, he headed off.

Mandy said, "Not everyone sees the value in what we're doing."

"Not everyone has to," Lucy said. "Just enough people to stop the storm."

Lucy and Mandy called out to everyone who passed by. Their pleas sounded muted in the rain. Some people scoffed, while others ignored them. A teenage girl sought shelter under the awning. Her name was Patricia, she said.

"Will this rain ever stop?" Patricia asked.

"You can help stop it," Lucy explained. "Let me show you how."

Lucy showed Patricia how to alter her WeatherPal. Patricia set her device to Sunny Weather. A sunbeam pierced the gloom right above their heads. Everywhere else stayed dark.

"This is awesome!" Patricia's eyes widened.

"Spread the word far and wide," Lucy said. "That is the only way to disable the system. We need a lot of users to help. Every second counts."

Happy Dancer beeped and spun. Little Leaf swung its arms like tree branches in wind.

"They're adorable," Patricia said, snapping photos.

Lucy beamed. "Thanks."

"Mind if I share these on my socials?" Patricia asked. "My posts could go viral."

Lucy said, "Remind them to switch their WeatherPals. With enough MyWeatherPals, we'll finally stop the storm."

"Sure." Patricia tapped away on her phone.

Chapter Seventeen

Lucy and Mandy called out to more passersby. Soon a crowd gathered. As rain pounded the roof of the Visitor Center, many people took shelter. Little Leaf and Happy Dancer became the center of attention. Everyone asked what the robots could do.

Lucy watched her robots kicking, spinning, and climbing as the audience stared.

"The real test is how they work outside," Lucy told them.

Her phone buzzed with texts from the Activ8rs. People were flocking from far and wide, even from New York City, to modify their devices.

"The storm is getting worse," Mandy said. "I don't see why. Shouldn't our work be having some effect?"

"Maybe we haven't done enough." Lucy's phone buzzed again. An unknown number.

"It's Robby. I saw your robots on the news. Heard about the MyWeatherPals. The storm's still raging, right? Can I help?"

"I don't want your help," Lucy exploded. "This whole mess is your fault!"

"I just want to support your message," Robby said. "Not change it."

"Tell me more."

"I have a network of scientist friends. They can spread the word with universities."

"OK." Lucy held the phone to her ear. "If you insist."

More people showed up, eager to modify their devices. Lucy and Mandy helped them. Soon, Lucy's hands ached.

"I'm exhausted," Mandy said.

Lucy and Mandy told everyone to help at least two friends. Everyone agreed and hurried off. The clouds parted, revealing glimpses of a brighter sky.

"It's working." Mandy gazed up. "The rain's slowing down!"

Lucy said, "I hope it holds."

Behind her, tires whirred. The Activ8rs parked their motorbikes and hugged Lucy.

"Seen the socials?" Jim asked. "Your bots are trending worldwide!"

He showed Lucy his phone. Videos of her robots flooded the screen. Mexico, France, Spain—their message crossed borders. The captions read, "Save the robots, and save Cooperstown! Choose Sunny Weather!"

Lucy basked in the warmth. The wind slowed. The trees stilled. Birdsong filled the air.

"We did it!" Lucy cheered as Mandy and the Activ8rs gathered. "Finally, we harnessed the power of the MyWeatherPals."

Everyone hugged. In the distance, music rang out. Drums banged. Someone strummed a guitar. The music stopped. Tom and the workers walked over, arm in arm.

"We're the Sunny Thunderstorms," Tom said. "We've made a band. We want Happy Dancer and Little Leaf to join us."

"What about the clapping and cheering?" Lucy asked.

"I'm sorry." Tom hung his head. "It was a mistake. We're relieved the storm's over."

The workers circled Lucy. "We've changed our minds," they said. "Seeing the storm get out of control…we don't want a repeat."

"That's fantastic." Lucy smiled. "How about a massive concert? The Activ8rs can handle the catering. We can thank everyone who switched to MyWeatherPals."

Susan appeared in the crowd, hopping to the music's beat.

"I'm thrilled the plan worked," she said. "And I was the first to change my device."

"Remember," Lucy said, "I owe you three MyWeatherPals."

"We'll settle that later."

Everyone set up tents and food stations. The weather was perfect, dry and pleasant. Happy Dancer and Little Leaf explored the park. Lucy's phone rang, showing Mike's name.

"Listen," Mike said. "I caught your robots on TV. Their performance was amazing. I've told the committee. You're on track to graduate."

"Really?"

"I'm so proud of you," Mike said. "I had my doubts. But you're a real scientist. Your research led to a creative solution. Congrats."

"Thanks." She wished she could hug him, too. "That means the world."

"We'll celebrate once you're back."

Lucy headed to the concert. Her phone buzzed again. Robby.

"You again?" she said with a smile.

"Glad to hear about your party," Robby said. "But there's a problem."

"What is it?"

"Rumors of other Booths. Same chips, new systems. Locations unknown. I need your help to track them down."

"What would I do?"

"First, locate the Booths and the chips. Then fix them or shut them off. I have scientists backing me. We have funding. But you've got the creativity."

"I don't know about that."

"Trust me. Will you and the Activ8rs join me?"

Lucy hung up and told the Activ8rs about the call.

"I'm not so sure," Tom said.

Mandy broke the silence. "Think of all the good we could do. And think of the chances to travel! I've always dreamt of flying to new places."

"Robby's not all bad," Lucy said. "You could take a break from your jobs."

Mandy gazed over to the concert. Jazz music rang out. "OK. Let's party first!"